Dance, Tanya

ISBN 0-590-45427-7

Text copyright © 1989 by Patricia Lee Gauch.
Illustrations copyright © 1989 by Satomi Ichikawa.
All rights reserved. Published by Scholastic Inc., 730 Broadway, New York, NY 10003,
by arrangement with Philomel Books, a division of The Putnam & Grosset Group.

12 11 10 9 8 7 6 5 4 3 2 1   1 2 3 4 5 6/9

Printed in the U.S.A.   08

First Scholastic printing, September 1991

SATOMI ICHIKAWA

Dance, Tanya

Story by PATRICIA LEE GAUCH

SCHOLASTIC INC.

NEW YORK   TORONTO   LONDON   AUCKLAND   SYDNEY

For Claudine and Anne
who love dance

Little Tanya loved to dance.

When her older sister Elise put on her leotards and slippers to practice,
Tanya put on her shirt and took off her shoes to practice too.

When Elise did her positions—first, second, fourth and fifth,
Tanya did too.

When Elise did a perfect *plié*, Tanya did too.

When Elise practiced her *pirouette* and *arabesque*, Tanya did the same.
Tanya particularly liked to do the arabesque.

Sometimes Tanya liked to dance alone,

or dance a *pas de deux* with her ballerina bear Barbara.

And when her mother put on *Swan Lake,* and Elise danced a whole song in arabesques and *jetés* right across the living room floor, Tanya put on her tutu and danced arabesques and jetés across the living room floor too. Tanya made a very good sad swan.

But when Elise went to her lesson, and
Tanya wanted to go too, her mother said,
"You're too little, Tanyette. Someday . . ."

And so sometimes Tanya would go along but only to watch her sister Elise and all of the other dancers through the big window, as they danced their arabesques and their jetés across the wide dance floor.

One day, when it was spring and the flowers were opening their eyes,
Elise got ready for a special dance recital.

She put on a new tutu with petals, and pink lipstick which she was never to use, and a dab of rouge on each cheek, and her mother combed her hair into a long, beautiful silky braid.

And everybody came to see Elise dance. Grandma and Grandpa from the country came. Aunt May who always wore a hat, and Uncle Ernie who never smiled came.

And Tanya came and tried to see over the man with the lumpy hat who sat right in front of her. By sitting on her feet, Tanya could see that Elise was a wonderful flower, doing her arabesques and her pliés just right.

And soon Tanya was very happy and sleepy as well.

"You have a dancer in your family," Aunt May whispered as the family left the large room with all of the hats and voices. Tanya did not even hear for she was fast asleep in her mother's arms.

But when they all got home and drank coffee and laughed and said what a good dancer Elise was, someone put on *Swan Lake* and Tanya woke up.

And while nobody was looking, Tanya found her tutu, and her scarf. And Tanya danced too. All alone.

The music played loud and sweet, and she did a plié and arabesque and five grands jetés right across the floor.

"Dance, Tanya," her sister said, and her mother held her breath. Grandma looked over her glasses. "You have two dancers in your family," she said. Everyone in the room clapped. Elise did too.

Tanya was such a wonderful sad swan.

"Bow, my Tanyette," her mother said, and Tanya bowed.

Then she crawled back up on her mother's lap, like a tired kitten, and went to sleep again.

But her mother did not forget. On Christmas morning
Tanya discovered a large package under the tree for her.
In it she found a shiny case, a pair of her own leotards,
and slippers just the right size.

"Come along, Tanyette," her mother said when it was time
to go to Elise's lesson. "Bring your case," her sister said, and
Tanya knew she wasn't too little anymore.